This igloo book belongs to:

igloobooks

Published in 2017
by Igloo Books Ltd
Cottage Farm
Sywell
NN6 0BJ
www.igloobooks.com

GUA006 0217
2 4 6 8 10 9 7 5 3 1
ISBN 978-1-78670-565-5

Based on the original story by Robert Louis Stevenson
Illustrated by Eva Morales
Written by Helen Catt

Cover designed by Lee Italiano
Interiors designed by Justine Ablett
and Katie Messenger
Edited by Hannah Cather

Printed and manufactured in China

Treasure Island

igloobooks

I am Jim Hawkins and my tale begins when I was a young boy, at my father's inn, the Admiral Benbow. It was there that I first met an old sailor called Billy Bones.

"Fifteen men on the dead man's chest. Yo-ho-ho and a bottle of rum!" Billy would sing, as he showed me an old treasure map. He told tales of pirates and the hidden treasure of the long-dead Captain Flint. **"It's the map the pirates want,"** Billy muttered.

Soon after, Billy died suddenly. It was then that I resolved to take his map and sail with my trusted friend, Captain Smollett, to find Treasure Island for myself.

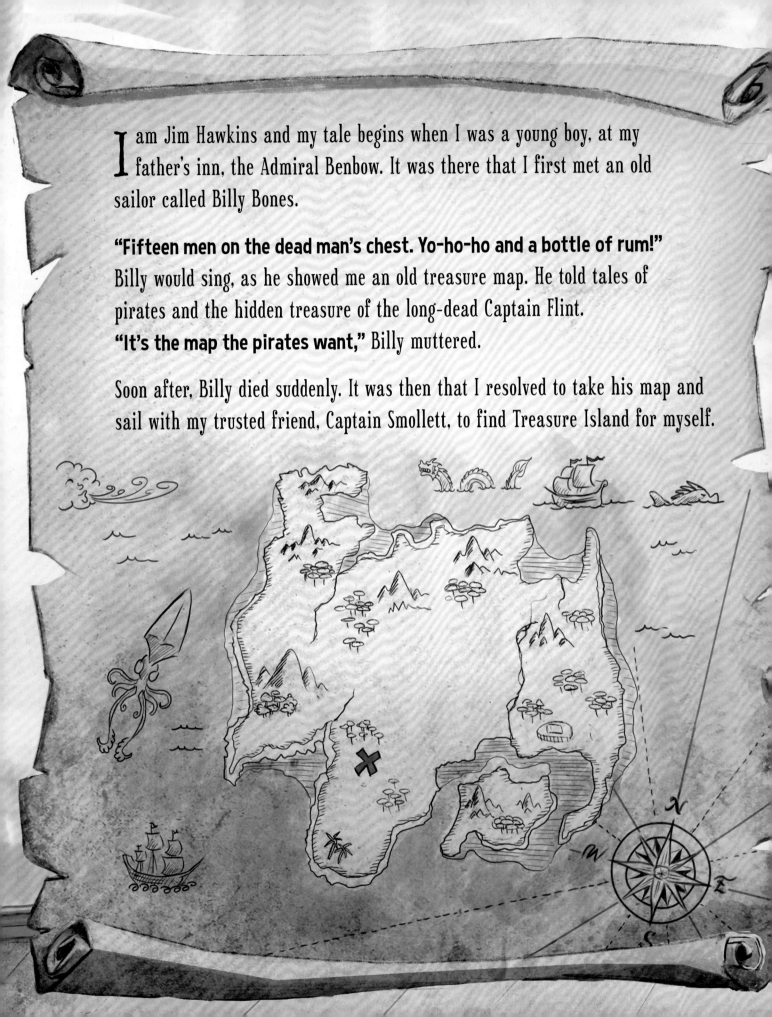

At Bristol docks, I saw the Hispaniola for the first time. I felt a thrill of excitement, but as I boarded, Captain Smollett beckoned me over.

"I don't trust this crew," he whispered to me.

Suddenly, a voice boomed behind us. It was that of Long John Silver. Billy Bones had warned me about this one-legged sailor.

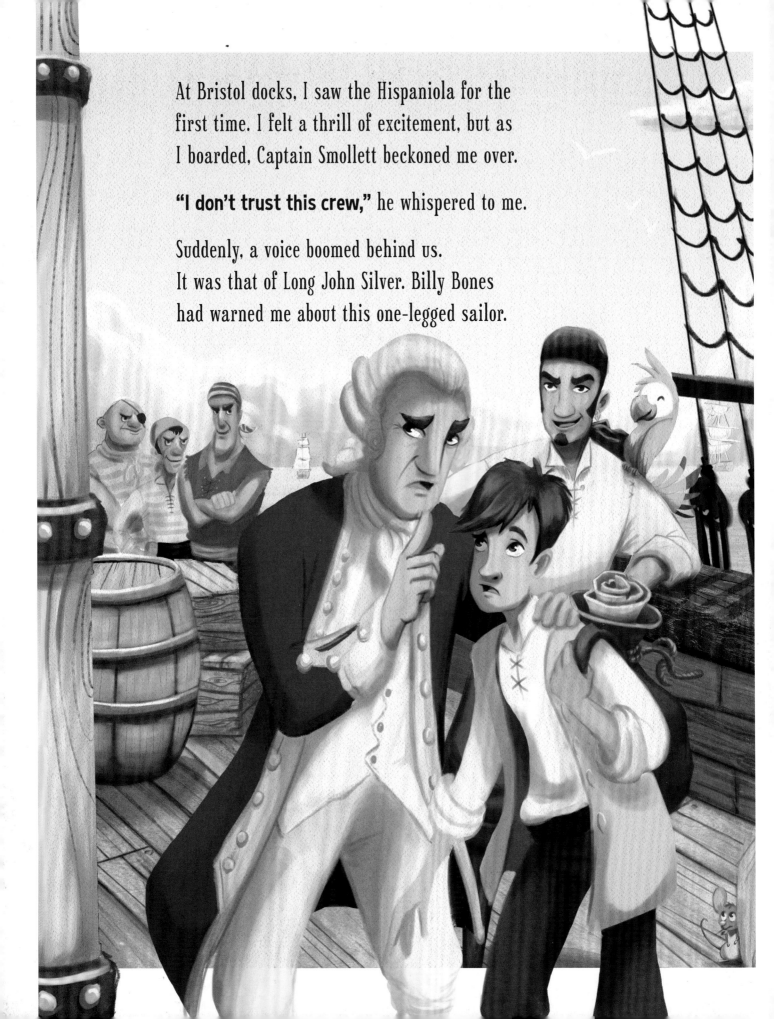

One day, whilst in the ship's kitchen, I heard Silver slyly whispering to another sailor. He didn't know I was there. **"Someone on this ship has the map to Flint's treasure,"** he hissed to the sailor. **"We were Flint's crew and it's ours by right. When we see land, you stay aboard and take the ship. I'll find the treasure."**

At that moment, the lookout in the crow's nest shouted, **"Land ahoy!"** We had found Treasure Island.

The crew scrambled on deck and I rushed to the helm to find Smollett. "Captain," I whispered. **"Silver is planning a mutiny."**

Smollett nodded and whispered to me, **"Don't worry, Jim, I have a plan."**

"Long John Silver!" shouted Smollett.

"Take some men and go ashore. We need water and supplies."

Determined to discover the pirates' plans, I hid in their boat as they cast off. As we neared the beach, Silver muttered threats against Smollett and the crew. Suddenly, he spotted me. In a panic, I dived into the water and swam to shore. I heard Silver shout after me, but I was too terrified to look back.

Once ashore, I ran to the forest to hide. I heard a strange rustling in the shadows. **"Who's there?"** I called, nervously. A man with a shaggy beard stepped forward. **"My name is Ben Gunn,"** he said, hoarsely. **"Pirates marooned me here years ago. That's not Flint's ship, is it?"** **"Flint is dead,"** I said, **"but his old crew are leading a mutiny."**

Ben agreed to help, if I promised him passage back home.

Ben led me along a marshy trail. On a craggy hill, I saw a British flag flying from a wooden fort. **"That'll be your friends,"** said Ben. I rushed inside and Ben followed. Smollett told us how, after Silver had gone ashore, the pirates left aboard mutinied. Those still loyal to Smollett escaped on a rowboat, which the pirates sunk with a cannonball. They had swum ashore, found Flint's old fort and set up camp there.

Suddenly, we heard pirates shout as they ran with their swords drawn.

"HOLD THE FORT!" Captain Smollett ordered. We each grabbed a cutlass, ready to fight. But we had forgotten that it was Flint's old crew who built the fort, and Silver knew a secret entrance.

The pirates swarmed through the hidden passage and Captain Smollett gave the order to flee. I turned to run with the others, but someone grabbed me roughly by the shirt and pulled me back.

"Captain!" I shouted, but no one heard me over the commotion.

"**Hello, Jim,**" said Silver. "**I believe you have something we want.**"
I struggled, but the pirate held me firm. "**You'll get nothing from me!**"
I cried, but as I spoke, another buccaneer took my knapsack and pulled
out the map. The pirates cheered and my heart sank to my boots.

"No hard feelings, Jim," Silver whispered, as we walked along the marshy path. "Now, let's make a deal. If one more thing goes wrong, these scurvy dogs will turn against me. But you're better than that. I'll stand by you and keep you safe, if, when the time comes, you stand by me."

We reached the grove where three tall pine trees stood, as shown on the map. All we found there was a hole in the ground, full of empty chests and cases. The pirates leapt into the pit, digging with their fingers, but found just a single two-guinea piece.

"Two guineas! That's all that's left of the treasure!"

one of the pirates shouted.

"That scoundrel brought us here for nothing, and now we'll be arrested and tried for mutiny."

They turned on us, with swords and cutlasses drawn.

"Run, Jim!"
shouted Silver.

Crack! Crack! Crack!

Three musket shots flashed out of the thicket and Smollett, Ben and the rest of the crew burst into the clearing.

The pirates scrambled out of the pit and drew their swords. Silver handed me one of his pistols and we took aim, ready to fire.

One by one, the pirates dropped their swords. They put their hands up and backed away, until they disappeared among the trees.

"Quick, men," Smollett said, "find their rowboats and destroy all but one. We can't have them going back to the ship."

The crew rushed off to obey his orders.

Later, I asked Ben what had happened to all the treasure. **"Follow me,"** said Ben, grinning.

We went to his cave, where, behind a little pool of clear water, glittered gold and silver bars, and thousands of unusual coins from all corners of the world. It was Flint's treasure.

In his lonely wanderings about the island, Ben had found the treasure and carried it to his cave. When Jim was kidnapped, Ben had told Smollett that the treasure was gone, and so Smollett and his men had hidden in wait at the grove, ready to ambush when the pirates arrived.

We gathered what we could and carried it to the ship. It was
weary work and when the sun started to set, we decided to
leave the rest behind. We had more than we could ever spend.

The mutinous pirates were left on the shore, marooned just as Ben had been. All except Silver, that was. We had made a deal to stand by one another. He had honoured that deal when we had discovered the missing treasure. Now it was my turn to stand by him, so when we set sail to England, he came with us.

Early one morning, while everyone was sleeping, I crept above deck and saw
Silver rowing away with a sack of coins at his feet. That was the last I ever
saw of him. I often see the island in my dreams. There is treasure still there,
in Ben Gunn's cave, but as long as I live, I'll never return to Treasure Island.